Also by Rachael Reed

Codefendant
Codefendant
Once a Cheater
Once a Cheater
Passport Bro
What Happens in Prison
Preference
Sprinkle Sprinkle
Championship Bad
Street Exodus
Street Exodus
Street Royalty
Pawns of Power
SIS
Cartel Bloodline
Get Money Girls
Skip the Games
Til Death Do Us Part
Backpage Hustle
Link in Bio
The Virgin and The Kingpin
A Gangsta's Heart
Boosters

Can't Turn a Hoe Into a Housewife

Sis

Sis
By Rachael Reed
Copyright © 2024 by Rachael Reed

Chapter 1: Ghetto Dreams

Jasmine stared out the cracked window of their small apartment in the projects, her mind wandering far beyond the grimy streets of Richmond. The sound of gunshots in the distance, the constant police sirens, and the ever-present scent of poverty were her reality, but her dreams soared higher than the dilapidated buildings that surrounded her.

"Jas, come help me with this," her mom called from the tiny kitchen, her voice weary from years of struggle.

"Coming, Ma," Jasmine replied, tearing her gaze away from the window. She walked into the kitchen where her mother was wrestling with a stubborn can opener, trying to prepare their dinner. Jasmine took the opener, her nimble fingers making quick work of the task.

"Thanks, baby," her mother sighed, smiling weakly. "I don't know what I'd do without you."

Jasmine forced a smile, but inside, she was fuming. Her mother, a strong woman who had raised her alone after her father abandoned them, deserved better. She deserved more than a life of scraping by, day after day, in these damn projects.

"One day, Ma, we're gonna get outta here," Jasmine said, her voice filled with a mix of determination and desperation.

Her mother just nodded, too tired to argue, too worn down to believe. Jasmine knew she had to be the one to make it happen. She had to find a way out, no matter what.

The next day, Jasmine walked through the neighborhood, her eyes sharp and observant. She saw the hustle, the deals going down in dark corners, the flashy cars that cruised through the hood, and the expensive clothes that adorned the bodies of those who had made it in the drug game. It was a dirty business, but it was a way out.

She spotted Jerome, a local dealer, leaning against a graffiti-covered wall, counting his cash. She knew him from school, knew he had dropped out to make money on the streets. Taking a deep breath, she approached him.

"Jerome, I need to talk to you," she said, trying to sound confident.

Jerome looked her up and down, a smirk on his face. "What's up, Jas? You lookin' to buy?"

"Nah, I wanna sell," she said, her voice steady.

Jerome raised an eyebrow. "You? Sellin'? Girl, you crazy."

"I'm serious. I need to make money, real money, to get me and my mom outta here. I know you can help me."

Jerome studied her for a moment, then shrugged. "Aight, but it ain't easy. You gotta be tough, smart. You think you can handle that?"

Jasmine nodded, her eyes fierce. "I know I can."

Jerome chuckled. "Aight then, meet me tomorrow at the park. We'll see what you got."

The next day, Jasmine was at the park early, her heart pounding with a mix of excitement and fear. Jerome showed up with a small bag of drugs and a rundown of the basics. She listened carefully, absorbing every word.

"Don't mess this up, Jas. This game ain't for the weak," Jerome warned, handing her the bag.

"I got this," Jasmine replied, her voice strong.

The first few deals were nerve-wracking, but Jasmine quickly adapted. She was smart, quick, and had a natural knack for the hustle. The money started to come in, and with it, a taste of the better life she had always dreamed of.

One evening, as she counted her earnings, her mother walked in and froze, her eyes wide with shock and fear. "Jas, what the hell is this?"

Jasmine looked up, her face calm. "It's money, Ma. Money to get us outta here."

"Are you dealin' drugs? Jesus, Jasmine, you can't be doin' this!" her mother cried, tears streaming down her face.

"I don't got a choice, Ma! This is the only way we can make it outta here. I won't let us live like this forever," Jasmine said, her voice breaking with emotion.

Her mother sank into a chair, covering her face with her hands. "Jas, I don't want this life for you. It's dangerous, it'll ruin you."

"I'm already ruined, Ma," Jasmine whispered. "But I ain't gonna stay ruined. I'm gonna make something of myself, no matter what."

The days turned into weeks, and Jasmine's reputation on the streets grew. She was tough, smart, and determined, qualities that caught the attention of Dre, the big drug lord in town. One day, while she was making a deal, a black SUV pulled up, and Dre stepped out, flanked by his crew.

"Jasmine, right?" Dre said, his voice smooth and commanding.

Jasmine nodded, her heart racing. "Yeah, that's me."

"I've been hearin' good things 'bout you. How'd you like to work with me? I can show you how to really make money."

Jasmine knew this was her chance, her ticket out of the ghetto. "I'm in," she said without hesitation.

Dre smiled, a glint of approval in his eyes. "Welcome to the team, Sis."

From that moment on, Jasmine's life changed. She was no longer just another girl from the projects. She was Dre's protégé, his right-hand, and together, they would take the drug game by storm.

But as Jasmine would soon learn, the higher you climb, the harder the fall. And in the world of drugs and money, trust is a luxury few can afford.

Chapter 2: Hustling Beginnings

Jasmine walked the familiar streets of her neighborhood, now seeing them through the eyes of a hustler. The corners she used to pass without a second thought were now potential business spots. She knew the risks—getting caught by the police, getting robbed, or worse—but the thought of the money and a way out of the projects kept her going.

She started small, working with Jerome to sell bags of weed and a little bit of coke. Jerome had given her a basic rundown, but out here on these streets, she was learning fast. The first few deals were shaky; her hands trembled as she handed over the goods and took the money, but she quickly found her rhythm.

"Yo, Jasmine! You got that fire?" a customer called out as she stood on the corner.

She turned, giving him a nod. "Yeah, I got you. What you need?"

The transactions were quick, almost routine after a while. Money exchanged hands, product moved, and Jasmine felt a rush every time a deal went down smoothly. But it wasn't always easy. The streets were dangerous, and not everyone was as friendly as her regulars.

One night, she was walking home, her pockets full of cash, when she felt a presence behind her. She quickened her pace, but the footsteps followed. Her heart pounded as she turned a corner, only to be confronted by a tall figure blocking her path.

"Yo, what you got for me, girl?" the man demanded, his eyes cold and menacing.

Jasmine's mind raced. She had heard about this—dealers getting robbed by their own customers. She had to think fast. "Ain't got nothin' for you, man. Just tryin' to get home."

"Don't lie to me," he growled, stepping closer. "I know you got cash. Hand it over, and you won't get hurt."

Her hands shook as she reached into her pocket, but she wasn't about to give up everything without a fight. As he reached for the money, she swung her knee up, hitting him square in the groin. He doubled over in pain, giving her just enough time to make a run for it.

Breathless and shaking, she made it home, slamming the door behind her. Her mother looked up from the couch, concern etched on her face. "Jas, you okay?"

Jasmine nodded, trying to steady her breathing. "Yeah, Ma. Just... had a rough night."

The dangers of the street were real, but so was the money. She counted her earnings, the crisp bills a reminder of why she was doing this. Each stack brought her closer to her dreams, to a life where her mother didn't have to struggle anymore.

As the weeks passed, Jasmine's confidence grew. She learned to watch her back, to keep an eye out for trouble. Her reputation spread, and soon she had a steady stream of customers. The money came in fast, and with it, the temptation to spend.

She bought her mother a new coat, something warm and stylish. "Jas, where'd you get the money for this?" her mother asked, suspicion creeping into her voice.

"Don't worry 'bout it, Ma. Just a little side hustle," Jasmine replied, avoiding her mother's gaze.

But it wasn't just about the money. The hustle gave her a sense of power, of control over her life. She was no longer just another girl from the projects; she was making a name for herself.

One day, while making a drop-off, she caught the attention of Dre. He was watching from his black SUV, his eyes tracking her movements. When she finished the deal, he called her over.

"Jasmine,?" he said, his voice smooth and commanding.

She nodded, trying to hide her nerves. "Yeah, whats up."

"I've been hearin' good things about you. You got real potential," Dre said, a smile playing on his lips.

Her heart raced. She was making waves and ready to move up the rank.

The next day, Jasmine found herself sitting in Dre's SUV, the luxury and power of the vehicle a stark contrast to her usual surroundings. Dre laid out his plans, offering her a higher position in his operation. It was risky, but the rewards were too great to pass up.

"You in?" Dre asked, his eyes locked on hers.

Jasmine nodded without hesitation. "I'm in."

From that moment on, Jasmine's life changed. She was no longer just hustling on the side; she was part of something bigger. Dre taught her the ropes, showing her how to maximize profits and minimize risks. They became a formidable team, and the money rolled in faster than she ever imagined.

But with success came new challenges. Jasmine had to navigate the treacherous waters of loyalty and betrayal, always watching her back. The lure of quick money was powerful, but so were the dangers that came with it.

As she climbed higher in the drug game, she realized that the stakes were getting higher, too. The line between friend and foe blurred, and she had to make tough decisions to protect herself and her newfound power. The hustle had become her life, and there was no turning back.

Chapter 3: Dre

Jasmine had heard whispers about Dre long before she ever met him. In the streets of Richmond, his name was spoken with a mix of fear and respect. He was the big dog, the one who called the shots, and his operation ran like a well-oiled machine. When Dre's black SUV rolled up next to her, she knew this was no ordinary drop.

Soon, Jasmine found herself standing in front of a luxurious apartment building, a stark contrast to the projects she called home. She took a deep breath and walked in, greeted by a large man who led her to an elevator. As the doors opened, she stepped into a world she had only seen in movies.

Dre's apartment was lavish, filled with expensive furniture, art, and the faint scent of money. He was sitting on a plush leather couch, casually sipping a drink. He motioned for her to sit.

"Welcome to my world, Sis," Dre said, using the nickname he would come to call her by.

"Nice place," Jasmine said, trying to mask her awe.

Dre leaned forward, his eyes locking onto hers. "I see potential in you, Jasmine. You got the drive, the smarts. But this game, it's bigger than you think. You ready for that?"

"I am," Jasmine replied without hesitation. "I'm ready to learn."

And learn she did. Dre took her under his wing, showing her the intricacies of the drug trade. He taught her about supply chains, distribution networks, and how to manage the money. He schooled her on street politics, the importance of loyalty, and the constant need to watch her back.

"You always gotta be ten steps ahead, Sis," Dre said one evening as they sat in his apartment, counting stacks of cash. "Trust is a luxury in this game. Don't ever forget that."

Their bond grew stronger with each passing day. Dre saw in Jasmine a younger version of himself, hungry for success and willing to do whatever it took to climb to the top. Jasmine admired Dre's intellect, his strategic mind, and his ability to command respect with just a look.

They became partners in crime, running operations together, from drug deals to elaborate scams. Jasmine's reputation grew, and with Dre's backing, she moved up the ranks quickly. The money flowed in, and with it, a taste of the life she had always dreamed of.

One night, as they were driving back from a successful deal, Dre turned to Jasmine. "You know, you're like a little sister to me. That's why I call you Sis. We're family now."

Jasmine felt a surge of emotion. Growing up, she had always longed for a sense of belonging, and here it was, in the most unlikely of places. "Thanks, Dre. Means a lot coming from you."

Dre nodded. "We gotta look out for each other. This game's ruthless. But together, we're unstoppable."

They celebrated their successes with lavish parties, expensive clothes, and luxury cars. Jasmine's mother noticed the change, the new clothes, the better food, but she didn't ask questions. Maybe she didn't want to know.

As Jasmine navigated her new life, she was constantly reminded of Dre's lessons. She saw the dark side of the drug trade, the violence, the betrayal, but she also saw the power and respect it brought. Dre's words echoed in her mind: trust is a luxury.

Their partnership wasn't without its challenges. Rival crews tried to muscle in on their territory, and there were close calls with the law.

But Dre always had a plan, a way to stay ahead. Jasmine learned to think like him, to anticipate moves and counter them with precision.

One evening, after a particularly close call with a rival crew, Dre and Jasmine sat in his apartment, nursing their wounds and counting their blessings.

"That was too close," Jasmine said, her voice tinged with fear.

Dre nodded, his expression serious. "This life, it's a constant battle. You gotta be ready for anything."

Jasmine looked at him, seeing not just her mentor, but a man who had been through the fire and come out the other side. "I'm ready, Dre. Whatever comes, I'm ready."

Dre smiled, a rare genuine smile. "That's my Sis. We're in this together."

As they toasted to their survival, Jasmine knew that their bond was unbreakable. They were more than partners; they were family. And in the ruthless world of the drug trade, that meant everything.

Chapter 4: Rise to Power

Jasmine stood on the corner of a dark alley, her eyes scanning the streets for any sign of trouble. She was a far cry from the girl who had timidly approached Jerome just months ago. Now, she was a force to be reckoned with, a name that commanded respect in the streets of Richmond. Under Dre's guidance, she had learned the art of the hustle, and she was damn good at it.

Their operations ran like a well-oiled machine. Jasmine and Dre were involved in everything from scamming credit card information to selling high-quality drugs. They had their hands in every pot, making money flow like water. The key to their success was diversification and ruthlessness. They knew when to strike and when to lay low, always staying one step ahead of the law and their rivals.

"Yo, Jas, you ready for this?" Dre asked, his voice low and serious.

"Always," Jasmine replied, a confident smirk on her lips.

Tonight's target was a rival crew's stash house. They had been watching it for weeks, learning the routines, the weaknesses. It was time to make their move. The plan was simple but effective: hit fast, hit hard, and get out before anyone knew what happened.

Dre and Jasmine moved through the shadows like predators. They reached the stash house, and with a swift kick, Dre busted the door open. Jasmine was right behind him, her gun drawn and ready. The guards inside barely had time to react before they were subdued, tied up, and left in a corner.

"Grab the cash and the dope," Dre ordered, his eyes scanning the room for any hidden threats.

Jasmine moved quickly, filling her bag with bundles of cash and packages of drugs. The adrenaline pumped through her veins, but she kept her cool. This was just another job, another step towards solidifying their power.

As they made their escape, Dre set a timer on a small device and tossed it into the room. A few minutes later, the stash house went up in flames, erasing any evidence of their presence. Back in Dre's SUV, they sped away, the glow of the fire lighting up the night sky behind them.

"That's how we do it, Sis," Dre said, a satisfied grin on his face.

"Yeah, we killed it," Jasmine replied, her heart still racing. "Can't Nobody Fuck With Us!"

Their reputation grew with each successful operation. Jasmine became known as Dre's right hand, a woman not to be underestimated. She had earned her place in the game through sweat, blood, and sheer determination. The streets whispered her name with a mix of fear and respect.

With the money rolling in, their lifestyle transformed. Dre bought a mansion on the outskirts of the city, a symbol of their success and power. The house was filled with expensive furniture, state-of-the-art electronics, and a constant stream of parties. Jasmine's closet overflowed with designer clothes and shoes, her wrist adorned with a diamond-studded watch.

One night, at one of their extravagant parties, Jasmine stood on the balcony, looking out over the city. She sipped champagne, the bubbles tickling her nose. Dre joined her, a cigar in hand.

"We've come a long way, huh?" Dre said, exhaling a plume of smoke.

"Yeah, we have," Jasmine agreed, her eyes reflecting the city lights. "But we ain't done yet. There's more to take."

Dre chuckled. "That's what I like to hear. Never settle."

The parties were a mix of business and pleasure. They networked, made deals, and expanded their empire. Jasmine rubbed shoulders with powerful figures, learning the intricacies of the drug trade at the highest levels. She was no longer just a player; she was becoming a queen in the game.

But with power came challenges. Rival crews tried to muscle in on their territory, and there were always whispers of betrayal. Jasmine and Dre handled each threat with precision and brutality. They sent a clear message: crossing them meant certain death.

One afternoon, Jasmine met with a supplier in a fancy downtown restaurant. She negotiated prices and delivery schedules with the ease of a seasoned professional. As they shook hands to seal the deal, the supplier leaned in.

"I've heard about you, Jasmine. You're making waves. But remember, trust is hard to come by in this business."

Jasmine smiled, her eyes cold. "Don't worry about me. I know who to trust and who to watch."

Back at the mansion, Jasmine and Dre counted the latest haul. The piles of cash were staggering, a testament to their dominance. But as they sat in the opulent living room, a tension hung in the air.

"We gotta stay sharp, Sis," Dre said, his tone serious. "The more power we get, the more enemies we make."

Jasmine nodded. "I know. But we ain't come this far to lose it all now."

Their bond was unbreakable, forged in the fires of their shared ambition. Dre had become more than a mentor; he was family. And Jasmine was determined to protect what they had built, no matter the cost.

As the night wore on, they celebrated their success, but the shadows of the streets were never far behind. Jasmine knew that the higher they climbed, the harder the fall. But for now, she reveled in the power, the respect, and the luxurious life she had fought so hard to achieve. The streets of Richmond Virginia were theirs, and Jasmine intended to keep it that way.

Chapter 5: Trust and Betrayal

Jasmine had always trusted Dre implicitly. He was her mentor, her protector, and the brother she never had. They moved through the dangerous streets of Richmond with an unspoken bond, relying on each other to stay ahead of the game. Dre had taught her everything she knew about hustling, dealing, and surviving. To her, he was untouchable, infallible.

One evening, after a successful run, they sat in Dre's mansion, counting stacks of cash. The lavish surroundings had become their norm, the signs of their hard-earned success. Jasmine looked at Dre with admiration. He had taken her under his wing when she was just a small-time hustler and turned her into a force to be reckoned with.

"Look at this, Dre," she said, holding up a wad of bills. "We're killin' it. Ain't nobody can touch us."

Dre nodded, a satisfied smile on his face. "We're just gettin' started, Sis. The sky's the limit."

But even in their moments of triumph, Jasmine couldn't shake a nagging feeling in the pit of her stomach. The streets had taught her to always be cautious, to always be on the lookout for the unexpected. She brushed it off, attributing it to paranoia from years of hustling.

One day, while making a routine drop-off, she ran into an old associate, Rico, who had been in the game for years. He was a shady character, but his information was usually reliable.

"Yo, Jasmine," Rico called out as she approached.

"What's up, Rico?" Jasmine replied, wary but curious.

Rico looked around nervously before speaking. "I gotta tell you somethin'. It's about Dre."

Jasmine's heart skipped a beat. "What about Dre?"

Rico leaned in closer, his voice low. "Word on the street is, Dre's been skimming off the top. He's gettin' greedy, Sis. Stealin' from you."

Jasmine's blood ran cold. "You better not be playin' with me, Rico. You know what happens to snitches."

Rico raised his hands in defense. "I ain't playin', Jasmine. I'm just tryin' to look out for you. You know how it is in this game. Trust nobody."

Jasmine walked away, her mind racing. Rico's words echoed in her head, planting the first seeds of doubt about Dre's loyalty. She couldn't believe it. Dre had always had her back, always been straight with her. But the streets were ruthless, and loyalty was a fragile thing.

That night, Jasmine lay in bed, staring at the ceiling. She replayed every interaction with Dre, every deal they had made. Could he really be stealing from her? The thought made her sick to her stomach. She had trusted him with everything, and the idea that he might betray her was unbearable.

Determined to find out the truth, Jasmine started to watch Dre more closely. She paid attention to the little things, discrepancies in the numbers, odd behaviors. The more she looked, the more she saw things that didn't add up. Her trust began to erode, replaced by suspicion and anger.

One evening, she decided to confront Dre. They were sitting in his mansion, the air thick with tension. Jasmine took a deep breath and spoke.

"Dre, I need to ask you somethin'. And I need you to be straight with me."

Dre looked at her, his eyes narrowing. "What's on your mind, Sis?"

"Rico told me you been skimming off the top, stealin' from me. Is it true?"

Dre's face hardened. "You listenin' to Rico now? That fool's just tryin' to stir up trouble."

Jasmine shook her head. "I don't know, Dre. I've been seein' things, things that don't add up. I need to know if I can still trust you."

Dre leaned forward, his eyes cold and intense. "You think I'd betray you, Jasmine? After everything we've been through?"

"I don't know what to think," Jasmine replied, her voice trembling with emotion. "I just need to know the truth."

Dre stood up, his expression dark. "The truth is, you're lettin' the streets get in your head. You know how it is out there. People wanna see us fall. They'll say anything to break us apart."

Jasmine looked into his eyes, searching for any sign of deceit. But Dre's gaze was steady, unwavering. For a moment, she wondered if she had been wrong, if Rico was just trying to mess with her.

But the doubt lingered. She couldn't shake the feeling that something was off. The bond she had with Dre was strong, but the seeds of mistrust had been planted, and they were starting to grow.

The days that followed were tense. Jasmine continued to watch Dre, her paranoia growing. She saw him meeting with people behind her back, making deals without her knowledge. The signs were there, and they pointed to betrayal.

One night, she overheard a conversation between Dre and one of his lieutenants. They were talking about a big score, but Dre was planning to cut her out of the deal. The realization hit her like a punch to the gut. Dre was betraying her, just as Rico had warned.

Jasmine's heart hardened. She had relied on Dre for so long, but now she saw him for what he was—a greedy, power-hungry man who would sell her out to save himself. The bond they had was shattered, replaced by a cold resolve to protect herself.

The first seeds of doubt had grown into a full-blown understanding. Jasmine knew she couldn't trust Dre anymore. The game had changed, and she had to adapt. She started making plans, quietly gathering allies, preparing for the moment when she would have to confront Dre and take control of her own destiny.

The streets were unforgiving, and Jasmine was ready to play the game on her terms. The rise to power had come with a price, and now it was time to collect.

Chapter 6: The Rival Crew

The streets of Richmond were buzzing with rumors. Word spread fast in the hood, and everyone knew that Jasmine and Dre had hit a major score by robbing one of the most feared crews in the city—the Black Knights. The Black Knights were known for their ruthlessness and their tight grip on the drug trade. They weren't the type to let a robbery slide.

Jasmine and Dre had pulled off the heist flawlessly, or so they thought. The money and product they had stolen put them on top, but it also painted a huge target on their backs. The Black Knights were out for blood, and the streets were about to become a war zone.

Jasmine sat in Dre's mansion, the tension palpable as she counted the latest batch of cash. Dre was pacing back and forth, his face set in a scowl. "We gotta be ready, Sis. The Black Knights ain't gonna take this lying down."

"I know," Jasmine replied, her voice steady. "We hit 'em hard, and now they want payback. But we got the money, the muscle. We can handle this."

Dre stopped pacing and looked at her, his eyes cold. "We need to lay low for a while, let the heat die down. But we gotta watch our backs. They could come at us any time, any place."

As the days passed, the tension only grew. Jasmine could feel the threat looming over them, a constant shadow that followed her every move. She noticed Dre's behavior becoming more erratic. He was meeting with people behind closed doors, making deals without her knowledge. Her suspicion grew, fueled by Rico's warning and the evidence she had seen.

One evening, Jasmine was out on the block when one of her associates, Tiny, approached her. "Yo, Jasmine, you heard about the Black Knights? They been makin' moves, lookin' for y'all."

"Yeah, I heard," Jasmine said, her jaw clenched. "They want revenge. We gotta be ready."

Tiny glanced around nervously. "Word is, they got inside info. Someone's been feedin' them details about your operations."

Jasmine's heart skipped a beat. "You think it's Dre?"

Tiny shrugged. "Could be. All I know is, someone's talkin', and it ain't good for you."

The seeds of doubt that had been planted were now growing into full-blown distrust. Jasmine knew she had to find out the truth. She started watching Dre more closely, noting every suspicious move, every secretive meeting.

One night, as she was heading back to her apartment, she noticed a car following her. She quickened her pace, turning down an alley, but the car sped up, blocking her path. The driver got out, and Jasmine recognized him instantly—Big Moe, one of the Black Knights' enforcers.

"Evenin', Jasmine," Big Moe said, his voice dripping with menace. "We got some unfinished business."

Jasmine's hand instinctively went to her waist, where she kept her gun. "What you want, Moe?"

"Just a chat," he replied, stepping closer. "You and Dre hit us hard. Now it's time to settle the score."

"I ain't got nothin' to say to you," Jasmine snapped, her eyes narrowing.

"Oh, I think you do," Moe said, pulling out a knife. "You see, we know Dre's been skimming off the top, and we know he's been plannin' to sell you out. He thinks handin' you over will save his skin."

Jasmine's blood ran cold. "You lyin'. Dre wouldn't do that."

Moe chuckled. "Believe what you want. But I got it on good authority that Dre's been makin' deals with our boss. You just a pawn in his game, Jasmine."

Jasmine backed away, her mind racing. She knew she had to get out of there, fast. She turned and ran, the sound of Moe's laughter echoing in her ears. She made it to her apartment, slamming the door behind her. Her hands were shaking as she called Dre.

"Dre, we need to talk," she said, trying to keep her voice steady.

"What's up, Sis?" Dre replied, his tone casual.

"Meet me at the spot. Now," Jasmine said, hanging up before he could respond.

She arrived at the abandoned warehouse where they often met for private discussions. Dre was already there, leaning against his car. "What's this about, Jasmine?"

"I ran into Big Moe tonight," she said, her eyes locking onto his. "He told me you been makin' deals with the Black Knights, plannin' to hand me over."

Dre's face remained impassive. "You really gonna believe Moe over me? We've been through too much together for you to doubt me like this."

"Then explain the meetings, the deals you been makin' behind my back," Jasmine demanded, her voice rising.

Dre stepped closer, his expression hardening. "I'm doin' what I gotta do to keep us safe. This ain't just about you, Jasmine. It's about all of us."

Jasmine's heart pounded in her chest. "I want the truth, Dre. Are you settin' me up?"

Dre's eyes flickered with something Jasmine couldn't quite place—guilt, maybe. "You need to trust me, Sis. I'm lookin' out for us, for our empire."

But Jasmine couldn't shake the feeling that Dre was hiding something. The once-solid foundation of trust between them was crumbling, and she knew she had to be prepared for whatever came next. The streets were closing in, and with enemies on all sides, Jasmine had to rely on her instincts and stay one step ahead.

The Black Knights were out for blood, and the betrayal from within was the deadliest threat of all. Jasmine knew that to survive, she would have to confront Dre and take control, before the streets claimed her life as their next victim.

Chapter 7: Betrayal Confirmed

Jasmine sat in her apartment, the hum of the city outside a stark contrast to the turmoil inside her mind. Big Moe's words haunted her, planting seeds of doubt that had grown into a gnawing suspicion. She needed proof—concrete evidence that Dre was betraying her. Her instincts screamed at her that something was off, and in the streets, instincts were everything.

The next morning, Jasmine decided to start digging. She began by checking their financial records, looking for any discrepancies. As she sifted through the numbers, she noticed small but consistent withdrawals that Dre had made without her knowledge. Her heart sank. The amounts weren't large enough to raise immediate red flags, but over time, they added up to a substantial sum.

Determined to find more, Jasmine turned to her crew. She approached Tiny, who had always been loyal and had a knack for getting information. "Tiny, I need you to do something for me. Keep it low-key, though."

"What's up, Jasmine?" Tiny asked, concern etched on his face.

"I need you to follow Dre. See who he's meeting, what he's doing. I need to know everything," Jasmine said, her voice steady but urgent.

Tiny nodded. "I got you. I'll find out what's goin' on."

Days turned into a tense waiting game. Jasmine continued to act normal around Dre, hiding her growing suspicion. Tiny kept her updated, but the information was slow to come. Finally, after a week, Tiny came to her with news.

"I saw Dre meetin' with one of the Black Knights," Tiny said, his voice low. "They were talkin' serious business. I couldn't hear everything, but it sounded like Dre's plannin' to hand someone over."

Jasmine's blood ran cold. "You sure about this, Tiny?"

Tiny nodded. "I wouldn't lie to you, Jasmine. Dre's up to somethin.'"

The pieces started falling into place. Dre's secretive meetings, the financial discrepancies, and now the confirmation that he was dealing with the Black Knights. Jasmine's heart ached with the betrayal, but she knew she couldn't let emotions cloud her judgment. She had to protect herself.

That night, Jasmine followed Dre, keeping her distance. She saw him enter a warehouse on the outskirts of the city. She waited, her nerves on edge, until she saw another car pull up. Big Moe stepped out, followed by two of his enforcers. Jasmine crept closer, her heart pounding in her ears, straining to hear their conversation.

"Dre, you better be right about this," Big Moe said, his voice dripping with menace. "You hand over Jasmine, and maybe we let you live. But you screw us over, and you're dead."

"I got it all planned out," Dre replied, his tone cold and calculating. "I'll lead her to you. She trusts me. Once you got her, the heat on me dies down, and we can go back to business."

Jasmine's breath caught in her throat. The betrayal was worse than she had imagined. Dre was not only stealing from her but was also planning to hand her over to save his own skin. Her mind raced, trying to process the gravity of the situation. She needed a plan, and fast.

She pulled back, retreating into the shadows, and made her way back to her apartment. Her mind was a whirlwind of emotions—anger, hurt, and a steely determination to survive. Dre had taught her well, but now she would use everything she had learned against him.

Jasmine called Tiny and a few trusted members of her crew. "We need to move. Dre's plannin' to hand me over to the Black Knights. We can't let that happen."

Tiny's eyes widened. "Damn, Jasmine. What do we do?"

"We take control," Jasmine said, her voice firm. "We hit Dre first. We take him out before he can take me out."

The plan was risky, but Jasmine had no choice. She couldn't trust Dre anymore, and she couldn't let him betray her. The next day, she gathered her crew at an abandoned building, laying out the plan.

"We hit Dre's mansion tonight," Jasmine said, her eyes hard. "We go in fast and take him by surprise. We can't let him know we're onto him."

As night fell, Jasmine and her crew moved through the shadows, approaching Dre's mansion. They positioned themselves around the building, waiting for her signal. Jasmine took a deep breath, steeling herself for what was about to come.

"Now," she whispered into her radio.

Her crew moved in, breaking down the doors and flooding into the mansion. Jasmine was right behind them, her gun drawn. They found Dre in his office, counting money.

"Jasmine, what the hell?" Dre exclaimed, his eyes wide with shock.

"It's over, Dre," Jasmine said, her voice cold. "I know what you've been doin'. Stealin' from me, plannin' to hand me over to the Black Knights. It's over."

Dre's face twisted with anger. "You don't know what you're talkin' about, Sis."

"Don't call me that," Jasmine snapped. "You betrayed me, Dre. You were like family, and you sold me out."

Dre reached for his gun, but Tiny was faster. He tackled Dre, pinning him to the ground. Jasmine stood over them, her hands steady despite the turmoil inside her.

"Jasmine, please," Dre begged. "I can explain."

"No, you can't," Jasmine said, her voice cold and final. "It's too late for that."

With a final, resolute look, Jasmine turned and walked out, leaving Dre to the mercy of her crew and the worst ass whooping he ever seen. She had made her choice. The bond of trust was shattered, and now she had to protect herself at all costs. The streets were ruthless, and Jasmine was ready to do whatever it took to survive.

Chapter 8: Strategic Moves

Jasmine sat in her dimly lit apartment, the events of the previous night playing over and over in her mind. Dre's betrayal was like a knife in her back, and the pain was still fresh. But Jasmine was no stranger to the harsh realities of the streets. She knew she had to move quickly if she wanted to survive and maintain her power. There was no room for hesitation.

"Alright, we gotta make moves, and we gotta make 'em fast," Jasmine said to Tiny and a few of her most trusted crew members. They gathered around her small kitchen table, their faces set with determination.

"We can't let NOBODY get the upper hand," Tiny agreed. "What's the plan?"

Jasmine leaned forward, her eyes cold and calculating. "First, we need to build alliances. There's strength in numbers. We need to reach out to other key players in the game, make sure they're on our side."

The crew nodded, understanding the importance of what she was saying. In the drug game, alliances could mean the difference between life and death. Jasmine had to ensure that she had enough support to counter any moves Dre or Dre's henchmen might make.

She started by contacting Marco, a well-known dealer with a reputation for loyalty and ruthlessness. Marco controlled a significant portion of the west side, and his support would be crucial.

"Marco, it's Jasmine. We need to talk," she said over the phone, her voice steady.

"Jasmine, heard you had some trouble with Dre," Marco replied, his tone neutral.

"Yeah, he's been skimming off the top and planning to hand me over to the Black Knights. I need allies, Marco. I need your help."

There was a pause on the other end of the line. "Meet me at the old warehouse tomorrow night. We'll talk."

Jasmine hung up, feeling a small sense of relief. Marco was a start, but she needed more. She spent the next few days reaching out to other key players in the game, securing meetings and discussing potential alliances. The streets buzzed with speculation about what Jasmine was up to, but she kept her moves quiet, ensuring that Dre remained in the dark.

As she built her network, the tension between her and Dre continued to escalate. They both knew that a confrontation was inevitable, and the streets were on edge, waiting for the clash that would determine who would come out on top.

One night, Jasmine received a message from one of her new allies, informing her of a secret meeting Dre had scheduled with the Black Knights. This was her chance to strike.

"We're gonna hit Dre at his meeting," Jasmine said, addressing her crew. "We need to send a message that we're not backing down."

The crew prepared for the raid, checking their weapons and planning their approach. Jasmine's heart pounded with a mix of fear and determination. This was the moment she had been preparing for. She had to be ready for anything.

As night fell, they made their way to the meeting location, an abandoned warehouse on the outskirts of the city. They positioned themselves around the building, waiting for Dre and the Black Knights to arrive.

When the cars pulled up, Jasmine gave the signal. Her crew moved in swiftly, taking out the guards and surrounding the meeting room. Jasmine burst through the door, her gun aimed at Dre.

"Dre, it's over!" she shouted, her voice echoing through the empty space.

Dre looked up, his face a mix of anger and surprise. "Jasmine, what the hell do you think you're doing?"

"I let you slide now I'm taking control," she replied, her eyes blazing with determination. "You betrayed me, Dre. You tried to sell me out. Now it's your turn to face the consequences."

The Black Knights stood back, watching the confrontation with interest. Their leader, Big Moe, stepped forward. "Looks like you got yourself a problem, Dre," he said, a smirk on his face.

Dre's eyes darted around the room, searching for an escape. But he knew he was trapped. "Jasmine, you don't want to do this. We can still work together."

Jasmine shook her head. "It's too late for that. You made your choice."

With a nod, she signaled to her crew. They moved in, taking Dre and his men a street hostages. Jasmine turned to Big Moe, her expression hard. "We're in control now. You can either work with us or get out of our way."

Big Moe studied her for a moment before nodding. "Alright, Jasmine. You've got guts. But we'll see how this plays out."

As the Black Knights left, Jasmine felt a weight lift off her shoulders. She had taken the first step in securing her position and eliminating the threat Dre posed. But she knew this was only the beginning. The streets were unforgiving, and she had to stay sharp to maintain her power.

Back at her apartment, Jasmine gathered her crew. "We did good tonight," she said, her voice filled with a mix of exhaustion and pride. "But this ain't over. We need to keep building our alliances, stay ahead of the game. Dre's out for now, but there will always be others looking to take us down."

Tiny nodded. "We're with you, Jasmine. Whatever it takes."

Jasmine looked around at her crew, her resolve strengthening. She had faced betrayal and come out on top, but she knew the battles were far from over. The game was ruthless, and she was ready to play it to win. With her new alliances and the support of her crew, Jasmine was determined to rise even higher, no matter the cost. The streets were her domain, and she intended to rule them with an iron fist.

Chapter 9: Confrontation

The air was thick with tension as Jasmine entered Dre's mansion. The lavish surroundings, once a symbol of their shared success, now felt like a stage for the impending showdown. She had spent weeks gathering evidence, building alliances, and preparing herself for this moment. Dre's betrayal cut deep, but her resolve was stronger than ever.

She sat in his office, his eyes fixed on a pile of cash. She was ready to handle business and reign as the head honcho in charge."

Jasmine closed the door behind her, her face set in a mask of determination. "She looked around and took it all in."

She leaned back in his chair, trying to maintain her composure. Feeling like she had to turn her back on one of the people she loved the most she felt a sense of power yet sadness.

Jasmine started to search through the records in Dre's desk that she couldn't access before and checked the money plays he had been making without her. She was going through it all.

Jasmine demanded, her heart pounding. "Why'd you do it? We were supposed to be in this together." She said to herself

The Black Knights were gunnin' for her and he was ready to hand her over. She was hurt and angry at the same time.

Jasmine felt a surge of rage. "You taught me everything I know, Dre. But you also taught me to never let anyone screw me over. And that includes you."

Jasmine looked up to the ceiling a single tear in her eye as she knew at that moment, she had to make the decision she didn't want to make. To make the call for them to take Dre out. He had been a hostage and tied up for days and she dreaded making the decision.

She grabbed her phone and made the call and with one simple line "Off Him" Dre was dead.

As she walked out of the mansion, the weight of her decision settled on her shoulders. Dre had been her mentor, her protector, but his betrayal had shown her the true nature of the game. There were no friends, only allies and enemies.

Outside, the night air was cool and crisp. Jasmine took a deep breath, feeling a sense of liberation. The confrontation had solidified her resolve. She was in control now, and she would stop at nothing to protect her empire.

Back at her apartment, Jasmine gathered her crew. "Dre's out of the picture. But we need to stay sharp. The Black Knights won't back down, and we gotta be ready for anything."

Tiny nodded. "We're with you, Jasmine. Whatever it takes."

Jasmine looked around at her crew, her family. They had stood by her, and now she had to lead them. The streets were unforgiving, but she was ready to face whatever came her way. Dre's betrayal had made her stronger, more determined. She had learned the hard way that trust was a luxury, and she would never be caught off guard again.

The next few weeks were a whirlwind of activity. Jasmine solidified her alliances, ensuring that her new partners were loyal and committed. She expanded her operations, taking over Dre's territories and securing her position at the top. The Black Knights made a few moves, but Jasmine's crew was ready, thwarting their efforts at every turn.

One evening, as she stood on the balcony of her apartment, looking out over the city, Jasmine felt a sense of pride. She had faced betrayal, but she had come out stronger. The game was ruthless, but she was ready to play it to the end. With her crew by her side and her resolve unshaken, Jasmine knew she could handle whatever the streets threw at her.

The confrontation with Dre had been a turning point, a harsh lesson in the realities of the drug game. But it had also been a reminder of her own strength and determination. As she looked out over the city, Jasmine knew one thing for sure: she would never let anyone take what was hers again.

Chapter 10: Taking Charge

The sun dipped below the horizon, casting long shadows over the streets of Richmond. Jasmine stood on the rooftop of her apartment building, the city sprawled out before her like a chessboard. She was ready to make her move, to take control of Dre's full operations and solidify her reign in the drug game.

The air was thick with anticipation as Jasmine gathered her most trusted crew members in the dimly lit basement of an abandoned warehouse. Tiny, Marco, and a few others who had proven their loyalty over the past few weeks stood around her, waiting for her to speak.

"Alright, listen up," Jasmine began, her voice firm and commanding. "We've been through a lot, but it's time to take charge. Dre's out, and we need to move fast to secure his full operations. We can't let anyone else swoop in and take what's ours."

Tiny nodded, his eyes serious. "What's the plan, Jasmine?"

Jasmine laid out a map of the city on the table, marking key locations that were critical to their success. "We hit these spots first. Dre's stash houses, his distribution centers, and his main headquarters. We take them over, and we show everyone that we're in control now."

Marco, a seasoned dealer with a reputation for being ruthless, spoke up. "You sure about this, Jasmine? Dre had a lot of loyal soldiers. They ain't gonna just roll over."

Jasmine met his gaze, her eyes steely. "We've got the numbers and the firepower. And we've got something Dre never had—loyalty. We move fast, hit hard, and take no prisoners. If anyone gets in our way, we handle them."

The crew murmured their agreement, the air charged with determination. Jasmine felt a surge of pride. She had earned their respect, and now it was time to prove that she was the leader they needed.

As they finalized their plans, Jasmine's mind raced with thoughts of the upcoming showdown. She knew it wouldn't be easy, but she was ready for the fight. She had to be. The streets were unforgiving, and any sign of weakness could mean the end.

The first target was one of Dre's main stash houses, a dilapidated building on the edge of the city. Jasmine and her crew approached under the cover of darkness, their movements swift and silent. They breached the building, quickly taking out the guards and securing the product.

"Move fast," Jasmine ordered, her voice low but urgent. "We need to be out of here before anyone notices."

They loaded the drugs into their vehicles, the tension palpable. Jasmine kept a close eye on her surroundings, her senses heightened. They couldn't afford any mistakes.

With the stash house secured, they moved on to the next target—a distribution center in the heart of the city. This one was more heavily guarded, but Jasmine's crew was prepared. They moved in with military precision, taking out the guards and securing the building.

As they worked, Jasmine's thoughts turned to Dre and all they had been through. He had been a powerful figure in the drug game for a long time, and his allies wouldn't just disappear. But she was ready for whatever came next.

The final target was Dre's main headquarters, a fortified mansion on the outskirts of the city. This was where the real battle would take place. Jasmine gathered her crew outside the gates, giving them a final pep talk.

"This is it," she said, her voice steady. "We take this place, and we take control. It might be some push back, but we're stronger. We're smarter. And we're more determined."

Tiny nodded, his face set with resolve. "We got your back, Jasmine. Let's do this."

They breached the gates, moving quickly and efficiently. The guards were ready, but Jasmine's crew was relentless. Gunfire echoed through the night as they fought their way into the mansion.

Inside, chaos reigned. Dre's soldiers were caught off guard, scrambling to defend their territory. Jasmine moved through the halls, her gun at the ready.

She found Dre's Lieutenant Mory in his office, surrounded by a few loyal guards. The room was a mess, papers and cash scattered everywhere. He looked up as she entered, his face a mask of anger and desperation.

"You think you can just take what's ours?" he snarled, reaching for his gun.

Jasmine fired first, the bullet striking him in the shoulder. "It's over, Mory you're done."

Mory staggered back, clutching his wound. "You'll never control this city, Jasmine. You're just a kid playin' a dangerous game."

Jasmine stepped forward, her eyes cold and unyielding. "I'm not a kid anymore. And this is my game now."

With a final, decisive shot, she ended it. Mory fell to the floor, the reign over. Jasmine turned to his remaining guards, her voice like steel. "You can join us or leave. But if you stay, you follow my rules."

One by one, they dropped their weapons, recognizing her authority. Jasmine's crew moved in, securing the mansion and taking control of Dre's operations.

As the sun began to rise, Jasmine stood on the balcony of the mansion, looking out over the city. She had done it. She had taken charge, and now the streets were hers. But she knew the battle was far from over. There would always be new challenges, new threats. But with her crew by her side and her resolve unshaken, Jasmine was ready for whatever came next.

The game was ruthless, but she was ready to play it to win. With her new allies and the support of her loyal crew, Jasmine was determined to rise even higher, no matter the cost. The streets were her domain, and she intended to rule them with an iron fist.

Chapter 11: Aftermath

The sun rose over Richmond, casting a pale light on the chaos that had unfolded the night before. The once-grand mansion that Dre had called home was now a battered warzone, littered with the remnants of the violent showdown. Jasmine stood in the center of it all, her body aching, her mind racing. She had emerged victorious, but the cost had been high.

Jasmine looked around at her crew, her eyes lingering on Tiny, who was being tended to by Marco. The others were nursing wounds, but they were alive. The sense of relief was tempered by the grim reality of their situation. They had won the battle, but the war was far from over.

"Alright, everyone, listen up," Jasmine called out, her voice carrying a note of authority. "We did it. Dre's out of the picture, but that means we got a lot of work to do. We need to clean up this mess and make sure we're ready for any retaliation."

Tiny, despite his injury, nodded. "We're with you, Jasmine. Whatever it takes."

The first order of business was to secure the mansion and the surrounding territory. Jasmine sent out scouts to ensure that the Black Knights weren't planning a counterattack. Meanwhile, she organized her crew to gather the weapons and drugs that had been scattered during the fight.

As they worked, the reality of Dre's downfall began to truly sink in. Jasmine had taken out one of the most powerful figures in the drug world, and the ripple effects were already being felt. Other crews were scrambling to figure out their next moves, and Jasmine knew that she had to act quickly to solidify her position as the new leader.

She gathered her key allies in the mansion's war room, a grim expression on her face. "We need to send a message," she said, her voice steady. "Let everyone know that I'm in charge now and that anyone who challenges us will meet the same fate as Dre."

Marco leaned forward, his eyes hard. "What about the Black Knights? They are a major threat."

Jasmine nodded. "We need to hit them before they can hit us. Show them that we're not to be messed with. Marco, I want you to lead that charge. Make sure they understand that we mean business."

Marco grinned, a predatory gleam in his eyes. "Consider it done."

As Marco and his team prepared for their mission, Jasmine turned her attention to the fallout within her own organization. Dre had left behind a power vacuum, and she needed to make sure that her crew remained loyal and focused. She called a meeting with her top lieutenants, laying out her vision for the future.

"We're gonna run this city," she said, her voice filled with conviction. "But we need to be smart about it. No more infighting, no more betrayals. We stick together, and we can take on anyone."

The lieutenants nodded, their expressions serious. They knew that Jasmine had proven herself in the heat of battle, and they were ready to follow her lead.

Over the next few days, Jasmine worked tirelessly to solidify her position. She met with other key players in the drug world, forging alliances and ensuring that her territory was secure. The news of Dre's downfall spread quickly, and Jasmine's name became synonymous with power and resilience.

One evening, as she sat in Dre's former office, Jasmine allowed herself a moment of reflection. She had come a long way from the girl who had started hustling on the streets to make ends meet. She had faced betrayal, violence, and unimaginable challenges, but she had emerged stronger than ever.

But the cost had been high. She thought of Tiny, recovering from his wounds, and the others who had been injured or killed in the fight. The streets were ruthless, and every victory came with a price.

As she stared out the window, Jasmine knew that the road ahead would be difficult. There would always be new threats, new challenges. But she was ready. She had the strength, the determination, and the support of her loyal crew.

A knock on the door interrupted her thoughts. Marco entered, a satisfied look on his face. "The Black Knights got the message," he said. "They're pullin' back, for now at least."

Jasmine nodded. "Good. But we can't let our guard down. We need to stay vigilant."

Marco grinned. "Don't worry, Jasmine. We got your back."

Jasmine stood, a sense of purpose filling her. "Alright, let's get to work. We've got a city to run."

As she walked through the halls of the mansion, now her headquarters, Jasmine felt a surge of pride. She had faced the worst that the streets could throw at her and come out on top. The aftermath of the showdown had tested her in ways she had never imagined, but she had proven herself as a leader.

The game was far from over, but Jasmine was ready for whatever came next. She knew that the challenges would keep coming, but she also knew that she had the strength and the support to face them head-on.

The streets of Richmond had a new ruler, and she was determined to build an empire that would stand the test of time.

With her crew by her side and her resolve unshaken, Jasmine was ready to take on the world.

Chapter 12: Rebuilding Trust

Jasmine knew that the battle was only half the war. The other half was the trust she needed to rebuild within her crew and her associates. The streets buzzed with the news of Dre's downfall, and everyone was watching to see how she would handle the aftermath. Trust was fragile in the drug game, and Jasmine was determined not to repeat Dre's mistakes.

"Listen up," Jasmine said, her voice echoing through the mansion's grand hall where her crew had gathered. "We've been through a lot, and we came out on top. But we can't afford to be complacent. We need to rebuild and strengthen our foundation."

Tiny, still recovering from his wounds but as loyal as ever, nodded. "We're with you, Jasmine. What's the plan?"

Jasmine looked around at the faces of her crew, many of whom had been with her since the beginning. She had to show them that she valued their loyalty and that she was different from Dre. "First, we need to tighten our security. No more slip-ups. Everyone needs to be on alert. Tiny, you'll handle that."

Tiny gave her a firm nod. "You got it."

"Second," Jasmine continued, "we need to make sure our operations run smoothly. That means no skimming, no double-dealing. We keep everything transparent. Marco, you're in charge of that."

Marco's eyes gleamed with determination. "I'll make sure everything's clean."

Jasmine took a deep breath. "And lastly, we need to show everyone that we're united. No more infighting. If anyone has a problem, they come to me. We solve it together."

The crew murmured their agreement, and Jasmine felt a surge of pride. She was their leader now, and she was determined to earn their trust every day.

Over the next few weeks, Jasmine worked tirelessly to implement her new strategies. She held regular meetings with her crew, ensuring that everyone was on the same page. She also reached out to her associates, reaffirming their alliances and addressing any concerns they might have had.

One evening, as Jasmine sat in her office going over the latest reports, Tiny walked in. "Jasmine, we got a problem," he said, his face serious.

Jasmine looked up, her eyes narrowing. "What is it?"

"One of the new recruits, Rico, he's been talking to the Black Knights. Looks like he's feeding them information."

Jasmine's heart sank. Trust was fragile, and betrayal was always a threat. "Bring him in," she said, her voice cold.

Rico was brought into the office, his face pale with fear. Jasmine stood, her eyes hard as steel. "You've been talking to the Black Knights?"

Rico stammered, "I... I didn't mean to, Jasmine. They threatened me. I didn't have a choice."

"There's always a choice," Jasmine snapped. "And you made the wrong one."

She turned to Tiny. "Take him out back. We need to make an example of him."

As Tiny dragged Rico away, Jasmine felt a pang of regret. She didn't enjoy the violence, but she knew it was necessary to maintain control. Trust had to be earned and protected, and sometimes that meant making hard decisions.

With Rico dealt with, Jasmine turned her focus back to strengthening her reign. She implemented new protocols for communication and security, ensuring that information flowed smoothly and securely. She also invested in new technology to monitor their operations and catch any potential threats early.

Jasmine's leadership style was different from Dre's. She valued loyalty and transparency, and she made sure her crew knew it. She held regular one-on-one meetings with her lieutenants, listening to their concerns and ideas. She also made it a point to reward loyalty, offering bonuses and promotions to those who had proven themselves.

One day, as Jasmine was going over plans for expanding their territory, Marco walked in. "Jasmine, I just wanted to say, you're doing a great job. The crew respects you, and they trust you."

Jasmine looked up, a small smile playing on her lips. "Thanks, Marco. It means a lot. But we can't let our guard down. There's always someone looking to take our place."

Marco nodded. "We know. But with you leading us, we're ready for whatever comes."

As the weeks turned into months, Jasmine's strategies began to pay off. Their operations ran smoothly, their territory expanded, and their reputation grew. Other crews saw them as a force to be reckoned with, and potential threats thought twice before making a move.

But Jasmine knew that trust was an ongoing process. She continued to work closely with her crew and associates, always striving to improve and strengthen their position. She also kept a close eye on the streets, ready to address any challenges that came their way.

One evening, as Jasmine sat on the balcony of the mansion, looking out over the city, she felt a sense of accomplishment. She had faced betrayal and violence, but she had emerged stronger. The challenges of leadership were immense, but she was ready to face them head-on.

The game was ruthless, but Jasmine had proven that she had the resilience and determination to succeed. With her loyal crew by her side and her strategies in place, she was ready to lead her empire to new heights. The streets of Richmond were hers, and she was determined to rule them with wisdom and strength.

Chapter 13: The Personal Cost

The night was quiet, the streets unusually still as Jasmine sat alone in her office. The dim light from her desk lamp cast long shadows, mirroring the darkness that had settled over her heart. The weight of her decisions and the ruthless world she now ruled pressed heavily on her shoulders. She had climbed to the top, but the journey had left scars—both visible and hidden.

Jasmine stared at the papers on her desk, her mind drifting back to the days when she first entered the game. She remembered the innocence she once had, the dreams of a better life for her and her mother. Those dreams had driven her into the drug trade, but the reality was far harsher than she had ever imagined.

She thought about Dre, the man who had been like a brother to her. His betrayal had cut deep, shattering her trust and forcing her to make decisions she never thought she would. Killing Dre had been necessary, but the memory haunted her. She had taken a life, and no amount of justification could erase the guilt that gnawed at her soul.

The door to her office creaked open, and Tiny stepped inside. "You okay, Jasmine?" he asked, his voice gentle.

Jasmine looked up, forcing a smile. "Yeah, just thinkin'. It's been a long road."

Tiny nodded, his eyes reflecting the same weariness she felt. "We've been through a lot. But we good now."

Jasmine leaned back in her chair, the exhaustion evident in her eyes. "Yeah, we did. But at what cost, Tiny? Look at what we've become."

Tiny sighed, sitting down across from her. "We did what we had to do, Jasmine. This life ain't easy. We knew that from the start."

"I know," Jasmine replied, her voice barely above a whisper. "But sometimes I wonder if it was worth it. All the bullshit, the betrayal. It changes you."

Tiny reached across the desk, placing a hand on hers. "We ain't the same people we were when we started. But we did what we had to do to survive. To protect what's ours."

As Tiny left the room, Jasmine's thoughts turned to her relationships outside the crew. Her mother had always been a pillar of strength, but Jasmine's descent into the drug world had strained their bond. She had promised her mother a better life, but at what cost?

One evening, Jasmine visited her mother's modest apartment. The woman who had raised her looked older than her years, the lines of worry etched deep into her face. Jasmine felt a pang of guilt as she hugged her mother tightly.

"How are you, Ma?" Jasmine asked, her voice soft.

"I'm managing," her mother replied, her eyes searching Jasmine's face. "But what about you? I worry about you every day, Jasmine. This life you're leading... it's dangerous."

Jasmine looked away, unable to meet her mother's eyes. "I know, Ma. But it's the only way I know to keep us safe. To give us a chance."

Her mother sighed, shaking her head. "I just want you to be safe, Jasmine. I want you to find happiness."

Happiness. The word felt foreign to Jasmine. She had spent so long fighting, surviving, that she had forgotten what it meant to be truly happy. The life she led was filled with danger and darkness, and the personal cost was becoming more apparent every day.

Back at the mansion, Jasmine found herself thinking about her father. The man who had abandoned her as a child, leaving her to navigate the harsh realities of the ghetto. She had vowed never to be like him, to be stronger, tougher. But in her quest for power, she had lost a part of herself.

She reached for the photo on her desk, a picture of her and her mother from happier times. Jasmine traced the outline of their faces, a lump forming in her throat. She had wanted to protect her mother, to give her a better life, but the price had been steep.

As she sat alone in the quiet of her office, Jasmine realized that the path she had chosen had isolated her. The relationships she had sacrificed, the trust she had lost—it all weighed heavily on her. The personal cost of her rise to power was immense, and the guilt and loss of innocence were burdens she would carry forever.

But despite the darkness, Jasmine knew she couldn't turn back. She had come too far, and there was no escaping the life she had built. The streets demanded everything, and she had given it all. Now, she had to live with the consequences of her choices.

Jasmine took a deep breath, steeling herself for the challenges ahead. The personal cost had been high, but she was determined to continue fighting, to protect her crew, and to ensure that her reign remained unchallenged. The streets of Richmond were hers, and she would rule them with unwavering strength, no matter the cost.

Chapter 14: New Threats

Jasmine stood on the balcony of her mansion, the city lights of Richmond flickering like stars beneath her. The empire she had fought so hard to build was thriving, but with growth came new challenges and enemies. The streets were never silent, and neither were the whispers of betrayal and power struggles within her crew. She knew the hardest battles were still ahead.

The first sign of trouble came from a new player in town, a gang called the Iron Serpents. They had been making moves, taking over small territories and challenging established crews. Jasmine had kept an eye on them, but their rapid rise was becoming a threat she couldn't ignore.

One evening, as Jasmine and Tiny reviewed the latest intel in her office, Marco burst in, his face grim. "We got a problem, Jasmine. The Iron Serpents hit one of our stash houses on the east side. Took everything."

Jasmine's jaw clenched. "Fuckkkkkk. They're getting bold."

"We need to hit back," Tiny said, his eyes blazing with anger. "Show them who's in charge."

Jasmine nodded, but she knew it wasn't just the Iron Serpents she had to worry about. Internal strife was brewing within her crew. The power vacuum left by Dre's fall had created tension, and some members were questioning her leadership.

Later that night, Jasmine called a meeting with her top lieutenants. The atmosphere was tense, and she could feel the undercurrents of discontent. "We need to address the Iron Serpents," Jasmine said, her voice firm. "They're trying to take what's ours. We can't let that happen."

"But what about the internal issues?" Marco interjected. "Some of the crew are saying you're losing your grip. They're talking about making a move."

Jasmine's eyes flashed with anger. "Who's talking?"

Marco hesitated. "There's been whispers. Some think you're too focused on the big picture and not on the crew."

Tiny shook his head. "Jasmine's done more for this crew than anyone. We need to stand united."

Jasmine took a deep breath. "Marco, I need names. We can't afford any division right now."

Marco nodded. "I'll find out who's behind it."

As the meeting ended, Jasmine felt the weight of leadership pressing down on her. She had to deal with the external threat of the Iron Serpents and the internal betrayal festering within her crew. The next few days were crucial.

The first step was to show the Iron Serpents that she wasn't to be trifled with. Jasmine organized a retaliatory strike, hitting one of their main operations. The attack was swift and brutal, leaving no doubt about who controlled the streets. But Jasmine knew it was only a temporary solution.

Back at the mansion, Marco approached her with the information she needed. "It's Delo and a few others. They've been meeting in secret, planning to take you down."

Jasmine's heart sank. Delo had always been ambitious, but she hadn't expected him to betray her. "Get them here. We need to deal with this now."

That evening, Delo and his conspirators were brought before Jasmine. The tension in the room was palpable as she faced them. "Delo, I hear you've been plotting against me."

Delo stood tall, defiance in his eyes. "You're losing your edge, Jasmine. The crew needs stronger leadership. Not No Bitch."

Jasmine's gaze was icy. "Stronger leadership? Or just a power grab?"

"We need someone who can keep us safe, who can handle the threats. You're too soft," Delo shot back.

Jasmine's anger flared. "Soft? You think what we did to Dre was soft? You think taking down the Iron Serpents was soft?"

The room was silent, the crew watching the confrontation with bated breath. Jasmine knew she had to assert her dominance, but she also needed to be strategic. "You want to lead, Delo? Let's see if you can handle the pressure."

With a swift motion, Jasmine drew her gun and fired, the bullet grazing Delo's arm. He gasped, clutching his wound as blood seeped through his fingers. "That's a warning. Next time, I won't miss."

Jasmine turned to the others. "Anyone else have doubts about my leadership?"

The room remained silent, fear and respect etched on every face. Jasmine holstered her gun, her voice calm but deadly. "We move forward united, or we fall apart. I won't tolerate betrayal."

As the meeting ended, Jasmine felt a mix of relief and exhaustion. She had quelled the immediate threat, but the battle for control was far from over. The Iron Serpents were still a looming danger, and trust within her crew was fragile.

Jasmine knew she had to adapt, to show her crew that she was strong enough to lead but also wise enough to listen. She implemented new strategies, involving her lieutenants in decision-making and ensuring that everyone felt valued and heard.

The days turned into weeks, and Jasmine worked tirelessly to maintain her position. The streets were a constant battlefield, and every move she made was scrutinized. But she had learned from her past mistakes, using every setback as a lesson to strengthen her reign.

One night, as she stood on the balcony, Jasmine reflected on the cost of power. The betrayals, the violence, the constant threat of danger—it was a heavy burden. But she also knew that she had come too far to turn back. The new threats and challenges were just part of the game, and she was determined to play it to the end.

With a steely resolve, Jasmine turned back to her empire. She would face the new threats head-on, protect her crew, and ensure that her reign remained unchallenged. The streets of Richmond were hers, and she would rule them with an iron fist, no matter the cost.

Chapter 15: Redemption and Regret

The streets of Richmond had a rhythm, a beat that Jasmine had grown accustomed to. She had fought her way to the top, and now, as the queen of her empire, she was faced with the duality of her existence. Power had come at a cost, and the weight of her actions bore down on her. Jasmine knew she needed to find a way to balance her criminal life with moments of compassion, seeking some form of redemption amidst the chaos.

One morning, Jasmine visited her mother's apartment, bringing groceries and a sense of normalcy that both cherished. Her mother greeted her with a warm hug, her eyes filled with love and concern. "Jasmine, it's so good to see you. How are you holding up?"

Jasmine forced a smile. "I'm managing, Ma. Just trying to keep everything in check."

Her mother's eyes softened. "You've done so much for us, Jasmine. But remember, there's always room to do good. To make a difference."

Jasmine nodded, the words resonating deep within her. She had the power to change things, not just through fear and control but through compassion and giving back. She decided it was time to act on that realization.

That afternoon, Jasmine drove through her old neighborhood, the place where her journey had begun. She saw the same struggles, the same faces, and the same hopelessness that had driven her into the drug game. She knew she couldn't change everything, but she could make a difference, however small.

Jasmine started by funding a local community center, a safe haven for kids who were at risk of falling into the same traps she had. She made sure the center had everything it needed—books, computers, sports equipment, and most importantly, mentors who could guide the youth towards a better path.

As she walked through the newly renovated center, Jasmine felt a sense of pride. This was her way of giving back, of trying to tip the scales of her actions towards something positive. She watched as the kids played basketball, their laughter echoing through the gym, and felt a flicker of hope.

But the road to redemption was not without its challenges. Jasmine still had to navigate the treacherous waters of her criminal empire. One evening, as she was reviewing plans with her crew, Marco approached her with news that weighed heavily on her mind.

"Jasmine, we got word that the Iron Serpents are planning another attack. They're not backing down," Marco said, his tone serious.

Jasmine sighed, the weight of leadership pressing down on her. "We need to be ready. Double the security at our key locations. We can't afford any more losses."

As the crew dispersed to carry out her orders, Jasmine sat alone in her office, the flickering light casting shadows that seemed to dance with her thoughts. She had built an empire, but the cost was ever-present. The lives lost, the betrayals, the constant threat of violence—they were the price she paid for power.

That night, Jasmine drove to the edge of the city, where the stars were visible beyond the smog and city lights. She parked her car and sat on the hood, staring up at the sky. The silence was a stark contrast to the chaos of her life. She thought about Dre, Rico, and all the others who had fallen in the pursuit of power. Regret gnawed at her, a constant reminder of the choices she had made.

As she sat there, a voice from the past echoed in her mind. It was Dre, his words haunting her. "You think you can do this without getting your hands dirty? This game changes you, Jasmine."

He had been right. The game had changed her. But she also knew that she had the power to change things, to seek redemption in her own way. She couldn't undo the past, but she could shape the future.

The next day, Jasmine visited her mother again, this time with a plan. "Ma, I want to do more for the community. I want to help the people who are struggling, like we did."

Her mother's eyes shone with pride. "That's the right path, Jasmine. You have the power to make a real difference."

Jasmine nodded, feeling a sense of purpose. She began funding scholarships for local students, providing food and shelter for the homeless, and supporting small businesses trying to survive in the harsh economic climate. She knew it wouldn't erase her past, but it was a start.

Despite her efforts, the shadows of her actions lingered. Jasmine often found herself awake at night, haunted by the faces of those she had hurt, the lives she had taken. She struggled with guilt, a constant companion that refused to leave.

But in those moments of darkness, she reminded herself of the good she was doing, the lives she was changing for the better. It was a delicate balance, a tightrope walk between redemption and regret. Jasmine knew she couldn't change who she was, but she could strive to be better, to use her power for something more than just control and fear.

As the days turned into weeks, Jasmine continued her dual path. She led her empire with an iron fist, ensuring its survival against new threats, while also seeking moments of compassion and giving back to her community. It was a difficult journey, filled with challenges and internal conflicts, but it was a path she was determined to walk.

In the end, Jasmine understood that redemption wasn't about erasing the past but about making different choices in the present. She had become a force to be reckoned with, both feared and respected, and she used that power to create change, however small. The streets of Richmond were her domain, and she ruled them with a complex blend of ruthlessness and compassion, seeking redemption in the only way she knew how.

Chapter 16: Final Battle

The air was electric with tension as Jasmine stood in her office, her fingers drumming against the mahogany desk. A new rival, an ambitious upstart named Viper, had emerged, challenging her authority and threatening to dismantle her empire. The whispers on the streets were growing louder, and Jasmine knew that a final, explosive confrontation was inevitable.

"Viper's been making moves," Tiny reported, his voice steady but laced with concern. "He's taken over two of our key distribution points. If we don't act now, we could lose everything."

Jasmine's eyes narrowed, a fierce determination settling over her. "We hit him first. Hard and fast. We can't let him think he can walk all over us."

Her crew nodded in agreement, the loyalty and resolve evident in their eyes. Jasmine had led them through countless battles, and they trusted her strategic brilliance and ruthless determination to see them through this one as well.

She gathered her top lieutenants in the war room, the map of Richmond spread out before them. "Viper's base of operations is here," Jasmine said, pointing to an abandoned warehouse on the south side. "We need to hit him where it hurts. Take out his supply lines, his enforcers, and then we go for him directly."

Marco, ever the strategist, leaned in. "We need to split our forces. Hit multiple targets at once to spread them thin. They won't see it coming."

Jasmine nodded. "Exactly. Tiny, you take a team and hit the south side. Marco, you handle the east. I'll lead the main assault on Viper's warehouse."

The plan was set, and as night fell, Jasmine's crew moved with a precision born of experience and necessity. They were a well-oiled machine, each member knowing their role and executing it flawlessly. Jasmine led the charge, her mind focused and sharp, every detail of the plan etched into her memory.

The assault on the warehouse was swift and brutal. Jasmine and her team breached the perimeter, moving silently through the shadows. The guards were taken out before they could raise an alarm, their bodies crumpling to the ground without a sound. Jasmine's heart pounded in her chest, the adrenaline fueling her every move.

Inside the warehouse, chaos erupted. Viper's men scrambled to defend their territory, but they were no match for Jasmine's crew. Gunfire echoed through the cavernous space, the air thick with the acrid smell of smoke and fear.

Jasmine moved with lethal grace, her gun a natural extension of her arm. She took down one enemy after another, her eyes always scanning for Viper. She found him near the back of the warehouse, surrounded by his closest lieutenants.

"Jasmine!" Viper sneered, his voice dripping with contempt. "You think you can take me down? This is my city now."

"Over my dead body," Jasmine shot back, her voice cold and resolute.

The final battle was intense, a blur of gunfire, shouts, and the clash of steel. Jasmine's crew fought with a fierce loyalty, their resolve unbroken. Marco and Tiny led their teams with precision, hitting Viper's supply lines and weakening his defenses.

Viper's men fell one by one, their desperate attempts to hold their ground futile against the onslaught. Jasmine pushed forward, her eyes locked on Viper. He fired at her, but she moved with the agility of a panther, dodging his bullets and returning fire with deadly accuracy.

The warehouse became a battlefield, the air thick with smoke and the acrid scent of gunpowder. Jasmine's heart pounded as she closed the distance between her and Viper. This was it—the final confrontation that would decide the future of her reign.

With a final, decisive move, Jasmine fired, the bullet finding its mark. Viper staggered back, a look of shock and rage on his face as he fell to the ground. His lieutenants, seeing their leader defeated, threw down their weapons and surrendered.

Jasmine stood over Viper's fallen form, her chest heaving with exertion. She had done it. The new rival that had threatened her empire was no more. She turned to her crew, their faces grim but victorious.

"We did it," Jasmine said, her voice carrying through the smoke-filled air. "We took him down."

The crew cheered, their loyalty and respect for Jasmine unwavering. She had led them through the fire and emerged stronger. But even in victory, Jasmine knew that the battle had taken its toll. The cost of power was high, and the scars of this final confrontation would linger.

As dawn broke over Richmond, Jasmine looked out over the city she had fought so hard to control. The streets were hers, but the price of that control weighed heavily on her shoulders. She had won the final battle, but the war for survival and dominance would never truly end.

Jasmine knew that she would continue to face challenges and threats, but she also knew that she had the strength, the determination, and the loyalty of her crew to face whatever came next. The game was ruthless, but Jasmine was ready to play it to the end, ruling her empire with an iron fist and a heart steeled by the battles she had fought and won.

Chapter 17: Closure

The sun was setting over Richmond, casting a golden hue over the city that had been Jasmine's battleground for so long. As she stood on the balcony of her mansion, the cool evening breeze carrying the distant sounds of the streets, Jasmine reflected on her tumultuous journey. The path she had chosen was littered with betrayal, violence, and moments of fleeting victory. It had shaped her into the formidable leader she was, but it had also left scars that would never fully heal.

Jasmine's thoughts wandered back to her beginnings, growing up in the harsh environment of the housing projects with her single mother. The struggles they faced, the hunger, and the constant fear had driven her to seek a better life by any means necessary. Her father's abandonment had left a void that she tried to fill with power and control. She remembered the first time she met Dre, how he had taken her under his wing and shown her the ropes of the drug game. The bond they formed, only to be shattered by betrayal, had taught her the harsh realities of trust in the streets.

She sighed, the weight of her past choices pressing down on her. She had fought her way to the top, but the cost had been high. Lives were lost, relationships strained, and innocence shattered. But amidst the darkness, there were glimmers of light. The community center she funded, the scholarships for local students, and the small businesses she supported were all part of her effort to give back, to balance the scales of her actions with moments of compassion.

The community was moving on, as communities always do. Some people remembered her reign with a mix of fear and respect, acknowledging the stability she had brought to the chaos. Others moved past it, seeing only the violence and turmoil that came with her rise to power. But Jasmine knew that she had left an indelible mark on Richmond, one that would be remembered for generations.

Tiny approached her, interrupting her thoughts. "Jasmine, you alright?"

She turned to him, a soft smile playing on her lips. "Yeah, Tiny. Just thinking about everything. How far we've come."

Tiny nodded, his eyes reflecting the same weariness and resolve she felt. "It's been a hell of a ride. But we made it."

Jasmine looked out over the city again, her mind filled with plans for the future. She knew that her position at the top was never guaranteed. The streets were always watching, always waiting for a moment of weakness. But Jasmine was determined to stay ahead, to continue ruling with the same strategic brilliance and ruthless determination that had brought her this far.

"We need to keep pushing forward," Jasmine said, her voice steady. "Expand our operations, strengthen our alliances, and keep an eye on any potential threats. We can't afford to get complacent."

Tiny nodded. "You got it, Jasmine."

As night fell, Jasmine gathered her crew for a meeting. The room was filled with familiar faces, those who had been with her through the toughest battles and the hardest decisions. They looked to her with respect and loyalty, ready to follow her lead.

"We've been through a lot," Jasmine began, her voice carrying the weight of her experiences. "We've faced enemies, both outside and within. But we've come out stronger. We've built something powerful here, something that can last. But we have to stay vigilant. The streets never let go, and we have to be ready for anything."

The crew nodded, their expressions serious. They knew the truth of her words. The game was never over, and there was always someone looking to take what they had built.

After the meeting, Jasmine returned to her office. She sat at her desk, looking at the map of Richmond that had guided so many of her decisions. Her eyes traced the familiar lines and boundaries, the territories she had fought to control. She felt a mix of pride and sadness, knowing that her journey had been both a triumph and a burden.

She thought about the future, about the legacy she wanted to leave. Jasmine had found a way to balance her criminal life with moments of compassion, and she wanted to continue that path. She planned to invest more in the community, to create opportunities for those who were trying to escape the cycle of poverty and violence. She knew it wouldn't erase her past, but it was a step towards something better.

As she sat in the quiet of her office, Jasmine felt a sense of closure. Her journey had been filled with highs and lows, but she had emerged as a leader, a force to be reckoned with. She had found a way to navigate the darkness and still find moments of light.

But she also knew that she could never let her guard down. The streets were unforgiving, and the price of power was constant vigilance. Jasmine was at the top, but she would always be watching her back, ready to defend her empire against any threat.

The night deepened, and Jasmine stepped out onto the balcony once more. She looked out over the city, the lights twinkling like stars. Richmond was hers, but it was also a part of her, shaping her into the woman she had become.

With a final deep breath, Jasmine felt a sense of peace. Her journey was far from over, but she was ready for whatever came next.

She had found her place in the world, and she would continue to rule with strength, compassion, and an unwavering determination to protect what was hers.

The streets never truly let go, but neither did Jasmine. She was a part of Richmond, and Richmond was a part of her, forever intertwined in a dance of power, survival, and the relentless pursuit of a better life.

Chapter 18: Unwanted Call

Jasmine was deep in thought, sitting in the dimly lit office in Dre's old mansion that was now her empire. She had just finished counting the night's take, the stacks of cash spread out on the table in front of her. Jasmine had worked hard for this—every single dollar, every single bloody cent. The streets didn't hand out respect easily, and Jasmine had taken hers by force.

She leaned back in her leather chair, exhaling a cloud of smoke from the blunt she'd been nursing for the past hour. It was her moment of peace, a brief escape from the chaos that constantly swirled around her. But in the back of her mind, Jasmine knew the calm never lasted long in the game she played.

Her phone buzzed on the table, interrupting her thoughts. Jasmine grabbed it, seeing her boy, Tiny's name flash across the screen. Tiny didn't call unless it was some shit, and Jasmine knew it. She answered, her voice steady but cold, "What it is, Tiny?"

There was a beat of silence on the other end, and then Tiny's voice, normally calm and collected, sounded shaky. "Jas... it's yo' mama."

Jasmine's heart skipped a beat, but she kept her voice cool. "What 'bout her? What's Up, Tiny."

Tiny took a deep breath, and Jasmine could hear the hesitation in his voice. "The Black Knights... they done got her, Jas. She... she gone."

It felt like the air got sucked outta the room. Jasmine's mind went blank for a second, the world around her fading into nothing but the words Tiny had just said. Her mama... gone? That wasn't possible.

Jasmine's mama was the strongest woman she knew. There was no way.

"Say that shit again," Jasmine demanded, her voice shaking now, her hand gripping the phone so tight her knuckles turned white.

"The Knights rolled up on her while she was at the corner store. Caught her slippin'. They did her dirty. Jas... she didn't make it."

Jasmine dropped the phone, her whole body going numb. Her boys rushed into the room, after the sound of the phone clattering to the floor. Jasmine's chest felt tight, like she couldn't breathe, like her heart was being squeezed by some invisible force. She couldn't move, couldn't think. All she could hear was Tiny's voice replaying in her head, over and over again, like a fucked-up loop. The Knights... she gone... they got her...

Marco, saw the look on Jasmine's face and rushed over. "Jas, what happened? You good?"

Jasmine didn't answer. Her vision blurred, the world spinning as she tried to make sense of what she'd just heard. But it didn't make sense. It couldn't. Her mama was supposed to be safe. Jasmine had made sure of it. She'd kept the streets away from her, kept the danger at bay. How could this happen?

Marco grabbed Jasmine's shoulders, shaking her slightly. "Jas! Jas, talk to me! What the fuck happened?"

Jasmine snapped out of it, her eyes locking onto Marco's. But there was no emotion there, just cold, hard rage. "Them Black Knights. They killed my mama."

The room went dead silent. Everyone in the spot knew what that meant. The Black Knights had just signed their death warrants. But the look in Jasmine's eyes was something different. This wasn't just business—this was personal. And everybody knew, when Jasmine made it personal, shit got real ugly real quick.

Marco let go of Jasmine and stepped back, knowing better than to try and console her. This wasn't the time for that. Jasmine didn't need no comfort—Jasmine needed blood.

Jasmine grabbed her gun off the table, the cold metal feeling right in her hands. She didn't say a word, just walked out the door, her crew following behind her. The streets outside were quiet, too quiet. Jasmine could feel the tension in the air, like the whole block knew what was about to go down. And maybe they did. Maybe the streets were already whispering about what the Black Knights had done. Maybe they knew Jasmine was about to unleash hell.

The drive to the corner store felt like a blur, the city lights passing by in a haze. Jasmine's mind was a storm, a mess of rage and grief, but she kept it together. She had to. There was no time to break down, no time to cry. That shit could come later. Right now, she needed to see it for herself, needed to confirm the nightmare that Tiny had just put in her head.

When Jasmine and her crew pulled up to the store, the flashing lights of the cop cars were already there, painting the scene in red and blue. Jasmine's heart pounded in her chest, but she kept her face blank, her eyes cold as she stepped out of the car. The crowd that had gathered parted as she walked through, the respect they had for Jasmine making them step back without a word.

Jasmine saw the yellow tape, the markers on the ground where the bullets had hit. But it wasn't real until Jasmine saw the body bag. Her breath caught in her throat, her legs feeling weak beneath her, but she forced herself to keep walking. She had to see. She had to know.

One of the cops, a young dude with a face too innocent for the shit he was dealing with, stepped in front of Jasmine. "Ma'am, you can't be here—"

Jasmine didn't even break stride, her eyes locked on the bag. "Get the fuck outta my way."

The cop hesitated, clearly not used to someone talking to him like that, but he must've seen the look in Jasmine's eyes because he stepped aside. Jasmine walked up to the bag, her whole body trembling as she knelt down. She reached out, her hand shaking, and unzipped the bag just enough to see. Just enough to confirm what Jasmine already knew in her heart.

Her mama's face, lifeless and pale, stared back at her, the cold reality of death hanging heavy in the air. Jasmine's vision blurred with tears, but she didn't let them fall. Couldn't. Jasmine wouldn't let nobody see her weak. Not even now.

Jasmine stood up, zipping the bag back up with a shaky hand. The rage that had been simmering inside Jasmine since the call now boiled over, a fury so intense Jasmine could barely contain it. The Black Knights had just made the biggest mistake of their lives. And Jasmine was gonna make sure they paid for it in blood.

Jasmine turned to her crew, her voice deadly calm. "We hittin' back tonight. I want every one of them niggas dead by sunrise."

Keisha nodded, the same cold fire in her eyes. "You got it, Jas. We ain't leavin' nobody breathin.'"

Jasmine's heart pounded in her chest, her thoughts a chaotic swirl of rage and grief. But even in the midst of the storm inside her, Jasmine knew one thing for sure—Jasmine was gonna make them pay. Jasmine was gonna make sure every last one of them felt the pain Jasmine was feeling right now. And when Jasmine was done, there wouldn't be a single Black Knight left to tell the tale.

As Jasmine got back in the car, her phone buzzed again. This time it was a text, just a single line from an unknown number: "You're next."

Jasmine's blood ran cold, but the fear quickly turned to anger. Let them come. Jasmine wasn't afraid. Not anymore. They could send whoever they wanted, try whatever they thought would break Jasmine. But Jasmine had just lost the only person Jasmine had left in this world, and Jasmine had nothing left to lose.

Jasmine's eyes narrowed as she looked out at the dark streets of the city Jasmine had once called hers. Jasmine knew these streets. Jasmine had run them, bled for them, built her empire on them. And now, Jasmine was gonna burn them to the ground.

The car sped off into the night, the tension thick, the air charged with the promise of violence. The Black Knights had no idea what was coming for them. But they'd know soon enough. Jasmine was coming, and Jasmine was bringing hell with her.

The night stretched on, the city lights flickering in the distance as the car cut through the darkness. Jasmine's grip tightened on the gun in Jasmine's lap, the weight of what Jasmine was about to do settling heavy on her shoulders. But there was no turning back now. Jasmine was committed, ready to see this through to the end.

Jasmine's phone buzzed again, but Jasmine ignored it, Jasmine's mind too focused on what was about to go down. Jasmine knew the risk Jasmine was taking, knew that the next few hours could be Jasmine's last. But Jasmine didn't care. Jasmine was ready to die if that's what it took to avenge her mama.

Don't miss out!

Visit the website below and you can sign up to receive emails whenever Rachael Reed publishes a new book. There's no charge and no obligation.

https://books2read.com/r/B-A-WXARB-GPKPD

BOOKS 2 READ

Connecting independent readers to independent writers.

Did you love *SIS*? Then you should read *Can't Turn a Hoe Into a Housewife*[1] by Rachael Reed!

In the gritty streets of the city, where loyalty is tested and danger lurks around every corner, Can't Turn a Hoe into a Housewife dives deep into the underbelly of urban life. Erica, a seasoned escort with a sharp mind and a guarded heart, dreams of escaping the fast life and finding something real. But in a world where money rules and trust is scarce, her journey ain't easy.

When Erica crosses paths with Quan, a man with a genuine heart and a promise of love, she sees a glimmer of hope. But leaving the game ain't simple, especially with a ruthless pimp like Lil Ron, who

1. https://books2read.com/u/4XdEN1

2. https://books2read.com/u/4XdEN1

ain't about to let his top girl go without a fight. As Erica tries to walk the line between her old life and a new beginning, Lil Ron tightens his grip, turning their lives into a deadly game of cat and mouse.

Can't Turn a Hoe into a Housewife is a tale of love, betrayal, and survival in a world where the streets don't play fair. With a dark, raw tone and a cast of characters struggling against their circumstances, this story is packed with twists, drama, and the harsh reality of street life. As Erica fights to break free and find redemption, the stakes get higher, and the danger becomes all too real.

In this urban fiction thriller, the line between right and wrong blurs, and every choice comes with a price. Will Erica escape the life that's bound her, or will the streets claim her for good? Get ready for a cliffhanging ride through the hood, where love ain't always enough to save you from your past.

Also by Rachael Reed

Codefendant
Codefendant
Once a Cheater
Once a Cheater
Passport Bro
What Happens in Prison
Preference
Sprinkle Sprinkle
Championship Bad
Street Exodus
Street Exodus
Street Royalty
Pawns of Power
SIS
Cartel Bloodline
Get Money Girls
Skip the Games
Til Death Do Us Part
Backpage Hustle
Link in Bio
The Virgin and The Kingpin
A Gangsta's Heart
Boosters

Can't Turn a Hoe Into a Housewife

* 9 7 9 8 2 2 7 7 8 5 5 0 3 *